WITH EAGLE'S WINGS

JOHN MARINELLI

PREFACE

I HAVE TAKEN PEN IN HAND to write this, my seventh book, that I may express the majesty and grace of our Lord Jesus Christ in and through actual events. There will be ups and downs, pitfalls and glory moments as my story unfolds.

This is a Christian fiction story based upon Biblical truth, logic and the experiences here-to-fore attributed to myself as the main character, narrator and author.

It is further my intent to show the hand of God at work and Divine revelation that, I hope, will encourage, inspire and bless the reader.

I shall write as the Spirit of God moves upon me. However, this is a co-authorship between the natural mind of man and the supernatural mind of Christ.

I believe that it was God that bestowed this gift of writing upon me. Therefore, I feel confident that He will continue His good work through me until the day I meet Him face to face.

I am honored that God would choose me to communicate in such a fashion as this. I claim no great literary prize or boast of any past accomplishments. I only labor in concert with my Savior as He reveals to me the ideas and concepts that are the essence of my story.

TABLE OF CONTENTS

INTRODUCTION

OUR STORY BEGINS WITH A 10-year old boy named Johnny Jones. He's ridding his bike down an old country road in a little neighborhood called London Bridge, Virginia. His bike was old, without fenders and worn tires. His chain slipped now and then as he stood up to peddle so he could go faster. His family was not poor but not rich either.

It was early morning at the little country grocery store where they dropped off the morning newspapers. Johnny was a newspaper delivery boy. He had to roll up each newspaper, rubber ban every one and stack them in his basket. Then it's off to his paper route tossing papers in yards everywhere. Over 50 papers in all had to be delivered every morning before school.

Johnny was one of ten lucky kids that could earn money selling and delivering newspapers. It gave him a feeling of selfworth as he had a job and was being responsible like his father. It also provided extra cash to buy soda pop, snacks and marbles.

Johnny loved to get into the big marble games just outside the country store. The other kids would bring their marbles and put them up for grabs. If you could shoot them out of the big circle drawn in the dirt, they were yours to keep.

Delivering newspapers wasn't the only business Johnny worked at. He also sold fruit door to door. He would first go up to a house in the neighborhood that had a pear or apple tree and ask if he could pick some for himself. Then he would sell the freshly picked fruit to his friends and neighbors.

Johnny also took his dad's lawn mower with the gas can on his handlebars and pulled it down the street as he rode his bike looking for a yard to cut. His going rate was $2.50 per yard without trimming. The summer of his 11th year was his best. He had 15 clients that required cutting every week.

Then there were the cookies, crackers and cola business to construction workers that were building houses. It was easy money because the workers were hot and the cola was a good cold drink break in the mid morning summer sun.

Life was good with extra money, friends and lots to do. There was hunting for giant frogs in the marsh along swamp road, playing baseball, swimming in the creek, building forts in the woods and dreaming about tomorrow. Johnny was soaring like an eagle.

But all that was lost when Johnny's parents told him that the family was going to move to Florida. His heart was broken. His world was crumbling before his eyes. He even had to leave his dog behind. Who Johnny was, as a 10-year old, changed from an eagle soaring in the heavens to a chicken in the barnyard. Johnny quickly got lost in the shuffle.

CHAPTER ONE
The Search For Self Identity

T HE TIME TO MOVE CAME a few months later. The move to Florida went into full swing. The house that Johnny spent most of his formative years in was sold. He was taken from his friends and beloved dog and moved with his brother and sister to a strange place where it never snowed, rarely even got cold and was full of people with no names.

Johnny and family now lived in a single wide trailer in a trailer park full of other displaced families that migrated south for various reasons that Johnny didn't know and could care less about.

Johnny often found himself sitting in an abandoned drive-in theatre thinking about the times when he was happy, like playing on his grandmother's wrap around porch; playing cars with his friends in the sand pile next to the road; building forts in the woods and playing shoot-en up with his friends. He also thought of the times when the cattails grew tall and when he and others dipped them in kerosene, lit them to make a torch and shot them into the night air with his 50-pound wooden bow.

Life was good then. Oh there were times that weren't so great like the night grandma's chicken coop burned down and all the little biddies were lost; And the time his little chicken, that he raised from a biddy, grew up and ended up on the dinner table; *(See Gallery of Poems... "The Little Chicken" on page 66)* Or the time his brother chased him around the yard holding a black snake in his hands; Or the afternoon when he was leaving his grandmother's house to cross over to his house and saw four big black snakes cooling themselves in the sand under grandma's back porch with their heads exposed and swaying in the breeze. These were scary things and yet they seemed normal.

Johnny was now in a South Florida Mobile Home Park with only memories to keep him cool in the summer night breeze. He would soon face a new elementary school full of kids, some of which lived in his park and had already laughed at him and called him names. He didn't know why but thought it might be his Virginia accent.

The joys of being King of The Wilderness in the woods next-door to his house in Virginia changed into being afraid of everything and everybody around him. He would have an up hill climb to regain the, "Eagle," status that fostered self-confidence.

It would take years before little Johnny would stand up and be free from all the hang-ups that grabbed at his soul in those days. He now saw himself as a chicken among chickens in the barnyard of life.

Johnny slowly developed an, "I can't do it" instead of an, "I can do it" attitude and finally stopped trying. He hid his low self-esteem by being vocally tough around other kids. He was all talk but very little action. He ran with a tough crowd of boys but never joined in on their law breaking stunts. He always found an excuse not to go along.

Johnny had lost himself. The Virginia country boy was suppressed and fell from prominence only to reveal an alternate selfish ego.

He did find one friend in the mobile home park that was younger but ok to hang with. They fished a lot off the nearby train trestle.

One day a freight train came barreling down the tracks while they were fishing on the trestle. It was too late for Johnny and his friend to run. The trestle was long and narrow. It was, jump into the water, 10-12 feet below or die when the train rushed by. However, Johnny had an idea.

He told his friend to lay his fishing rod down on the railroad cross walk where they were sitting and lean forward as far as he could without falling. Johnny did the same.

The trestle began to shake as the train approached and the wind from the train pushed at the two boys as it rushed by missing them by only inches. The danger was over and the boys went back to fishing but never stayed on the trestle again when they heard or saw a train coming. Johnny still quivers when he hears a train whistle.

Just as Johnny was starting to make a few friends, his parents again moved the family to a new housing development north of where they were. It was far enough to lose touch with the few friends he had. Once again Johnny was faced with a new school and new kids to deal with. His mind raced with questions like "Will they like me?" "How do I fit in?" and "How can I hide if they reject me?"

Johnny went from living in a singlewide trailer to a three-bedroom one-bath home with a carport. He still had to share a bedroom with his older brother but it was better than the mobile home.

Johnny liked the new house. He helped his dad sprig the yard with grass and watered it until it grew into a yard. He planted a coconut in the sandy yard and watched over the months as a little coconut tree rose from the ground.

The coconut grew tall over the next few years and seemed to

represent Johnny's own rapid growth spurt as he entered his teen years. That summer, Johnny went from 5'6" to 6'1" becoming the tallest in the family.

Johnny's dad secured employment as a police officer in the town where their new home was built. Johnny was now entering the 7th grade and pushing 13 years old. When the new kids found out that Johnny's dad was a cop, they left him alone for a while.

CHAPTER TWO
A Splash of Love

JOHNNY SPENT A LOT OF time in the school library, mostly during his lunch hour. He retreated to the library so he didn't have to face the new kids who had already formed clicks and friendships that did not include him.

Rejection was to be the norm for that school year and two others as he was once again assigned to a new school by the school board based upon his address.

The 8th and 9th grads were spent in portable classrooms on a sandy lot. Then it was back to senior high at the original location only to face all the kids that rejected him in the 7th grade.

Johnny did have friends but they were not the "In Crowd." They were mostly troublemakers and slow learners. He got use to being and thinking that he was one of them. It was like looking at an eagle sitting in the barnyard with the chickens. He acted like a chicken but because he was an eagle, he just didn't fit in.

Then there was the public school curriculum that introduced a new theory of the origins of man called Evolution. It was only a theory but it was taught as scientific fact.

Creationism was pushed aside. With it came the demise of morality; the death of God and the end of normal life. Those who still believed in God and the Biblical account of creation were seen as fanatics, fools and dilberts. The truth was replaced with a lie and those that opposed it were put down and criticized.

So Johnny, in order to fit in, accepted the lie and turned from his convictions to being a liberal thinker. It was easy. As society ran wild with free love, casual sex, homosexuality and all sorts of immorality, Johnny found a semblance of acceptance, as long as he fell into the pecking order and stayed a chicken. It just didn't occur to him that he was really an eagle. Those days were over.

Johnny's search for his inner self crashed upon the rocks of hopelessness. He originally thought that when he grew up he would discover the reason he was placed upon planet earth at this time and in this generation. Instead, he embraced the notion that there was no purpose or divine destiny for him or anyone else.

He began to see human life as no more value than the smallest animal without the power to think or reason. He often would say to himself, *"Is that all there is?"* He just couldn't see the point of having any ambition, a will to succeed or a purpose for which to aspire. He often contemplated suicide.

Johnny was not an unusual case. There were many in his generation that felt the same way. Thus emerged the "Hippie"; the "Slacker"; and the "Self Absorbed" most of which turned to politics and other liberal platforms where they could rule over the masses. Self-exaltation was their goal because they believed there was no afterlife or eternal judgment. They rejected even the concept of God.

However, God had His hand on Johnny and did not abandon him. He called Johnny to himself in a Baptist Vacation Bible School when Johnny was eight years old. It was there that little Johnny Jones gave his heart to God and accepted Jesus Christ as his savior.

Johnny responded to an open invitation to accept Jesus, was baptized and made a member of the church. The small country church did not have a follow-up program of religious education and Johnny fell through the cracks and was lost in the things of the world.

Never the less, God did not give up on Johnny. He made a way where there was no way. *(See Gallery of Poems… "The "Way Maker""" on page 78)* He splashed him with His love and used the rejection from others to draw him back into the library where he was led to the Bible.

Every day Johnny would open the Bible and read as he sat by himself off in a corner. It was there that he began to hear the voice of God in scripture verses. It was as though the words written in the Bible jumped off the page and right into his heart. *(See gallery of poems… "Our Time of Prayer" on page 88)* He discovered his purpose and destiny. He realized that he was in fact an eagle and not a chicken. He began to fly. His inner self was healed and his life began to change.

CHAPTER THREE
Soaring Like A Eagle

Little Johnny Jones found himself in God but still had one foot in the world. Every time he tried to soar like an eagle the lust of the flesh, the lust of the eye and the pride of life would pull him back into the barnyard with the chickens. Johnny was in the valley of decision between heaven and hell. He wanted to follow God but needed the praises of men to feel like a, "Somebody."

Eternal salvation fell to the back of Johnny's mind. God was assigned to a small corner of his heart and consulted only in desperate times. Johnny didn't realize that to soar like an eagle he needed a mighty rushing wind that could only be found in God's Holy Spirit. The energy of self was not sufficient to attain lift off. It had to be *"A Splash of Love"* like before when he was 8-years old when it welled up inside until it overflowed and engulfed his very being.

There could be no more one-foot here and the other there. It had to be an all or nothing decision. Johnny had to decide to really follow after the things of the Lord or settle for being a wounded eagle that would never soar above the clouds again. *(See gallery of poems... "Beyond The Rainbow" on page 86)*

But Johnny was only sixteen. He had his own car, such as it was. He was just starting to date and liked the idea of chasing after girls. He finally made some friends. Little did he know that his friends hung around because he had a car and they didn't. He also didn't know, at the time, that his invitations to card games were because he was a good mark. He almost always lost at poker and always had some money to lose.

So Johnny made it through high school by the skin of his teeth and for the moment forgot about trying to *soar like an eagle*. He still had that nagging thought inside that he was just not good enough.

The "I can do" attitude never emerged. Johnny felt like he could not do anything good and that he was just a chicken among other chickens.

Johnny never took the college prep courses as the other kids did. He had no long-term goals and had no idea what or who he would be after graduation.

As many of the other kids went off to college, Johnny settled for looking for a job, but what kind of job? He had no skill set, no experience and no real people skills. He finally found a part time job in a men's clothing store as a salesman. It was after school and on weekends. Strangely enough, God was still with Johnny working everything together for his good.

The sales job taught Johnny how to deal with different folks and how to treat people nice. He even found himself being kind to others when they were not kind to him. In sales, the customer was always right. Certain qualities began to emerge that Johnny didn't know he possessed. He hoped that after school he would move up from a simple floor salesman to the assistant store manger. Johnny liked the idea of taking on more responsibility. It suited him. He liked to be in charge and tell others what to do but for now he was content to stay hidden in the shadows.

CHAPTER FOUR

The Call To Glory

JOHNNY EXCELLED IN HIS ABILITY to sell things. He was good at what he did. However, the men's clothing business was a six-day a week job with little pay and poor benefits. He quickly realized that it was a nowhere job. Unfortunately there was nowhere else to go. The economy was on a decline and jobs were hard to find. So Johnny settled for what he had and tried to be content. As he grew closer to the Lord through reading his Bible and personal prayer, he came to hate sales as it often put him in a position to exaggerate the quality and benefits of the products he sold.

God opened Johnny's eyes and he began to see the hand of the Lord in his life; how he healed him from a brain hemorrhage when he was just a baby; how he gave him wisdom to recognize the evil actions of his friends that before were no big deal; and specifically to know the will of God for him without a shadow of a doubt.

Johnny's heart was softening and his mind was being renewed. He still spent many a day in the school library but now looked forward to hearing the voice of God. He was still rejected by most of the, "In Crowd" but for some reason it didn't matter anymore.

High school came and went, Johnny found his way to and from work and then came the Vietnam War. Johnny was 20-years old and a prime candidate for the draft. News reports showed American soldiers being killed every day in ground combat firefights.

So Johnny decided to play it safe and joined the Navy where he was sure to never have to fight on land. He ran from a 2-year draft into a 4-year enlistment.

Once in the Navy, Johnny realized that the Navy also went to Vietnam and often fought as part of a landing party to assist Special Forces. But he was safe for the moment steaming in circles on a cruiser off the Atlantic coast.

It was while on the Navy ship that Johnny's loyalty to God was tested. At first he ran with his shipmates to bars and clubs when in port but now, as a full fledged Christian, he had to make a choice between following the teaching of Jesus or running with his shipmates down a road that ultimately would lead to his destruction. It was…reject his shipmates or reject God.

As Johnny prayed and read his Bible, he came across a scripture passage where Jesus was telling His disciples, *"He that is not for me is against me."* There was no in-between, no neutral ground. He had to go on with the Lord or fall away into a world system that was ruled by sin and condemned by God.

So Johnny backed away from his shipmates when they wanted him to go bar hopping. Again came the rejection and ridicule because Johnny wanted to serve the Lord. He tried to explain why but that made his shipmates even more angry. Some even said that Johnny was using God as a crutch because he could not be his own man. Their observations were somewhat true. Johnny was tired of making so many wrong decisions and life was too complex to absorb and manage it successfully.

Every time he tried, he fell into sin and guilt because he knew that his decisions were not in accordance with the will of his Heavenly Father. It made him sad when he tried to rule over his own affairs. Johnny's peace of mind and joy came from allowing Jesus to be Lord and seeking to do His will. That's where his heart was…to serve the Lord.

Johnny's test of loyalty was the 1st step in once again soaring like an eagle. He could feel the wind of the Holy Spirit lifting him higher and higher into God's glory. Johnny was actually experiencing fellowship with his creator. That, *"Splash of Love,"* that fell upon him so many years ago became a flood and with it came peace, joy, longsuffering, kindness and many other Godly attributes. He was being filled to even the over flowing of his spirit with the glorious presence of God.

Three years, eleven months and twenty-nine days came and went without incident. Johnny was discharged honorably from military service and returned to civilian life. Johnny was now 24-years old.

"Now what?" That's what zipped past Johnny's head. No job, no place to live, except with mom & dad and very little cash, only a few hundred mustering out bucks. No acquired skills from the Navy that could apply to civilian life. Swabbing the deck and saying, "Yes Sir" to officers had no real significance in Johnny's new world.

So, Johnny went back to that which he hated most, "Sales." He jumped into an assistant manager's position that paid a little more but brought with it more responsibility. He now had to work four nights a week and had to do the daily receipts after closing.

However, God had not forgotten Johnny. He was called to glory for a very special destiny. He knew that but didn't know when or exactly what destiny would play out in his life. It took a year and a half of sales and management before Johnny was ready to move on with God.

Meanwhile, Johnny went to church; several home fellowship meetings; two Bible studies and a weekly prayer session. He began praying for others and teaching in his own age group. He witnessed to the lost and downtrodden as he could. He slowly began to find himself in God. *(See Gallery of Poems… "I Find Myself In God" on page 74)*

Johnny was now 26-years old. He still found that some people around him rejected him. This troubled Johnny as he was now in a church family where everyone was suppose to be acceptant of each other. Instead, Johnny found jealousy, infighting, gossip and pretend Christianity. Needless to say, Johnny was extremely disappointed.

CHAPTER FIVE
The Midnight Dream

THE CHURCH THAT JOHNNY SUPPORTED was on fire for God, even though it had factions of discontent running through it. There was an explosion of growth and spirituality. Revival was breaking out everywhere. Johnny signed up for participation in a weeklong camp meeting where guest speakers came to preach and minister to church family and friends.

Half way through the 3rd evening session, the speaker began talking about God wanting Christian Soldiers that would do battle in the spirit with evil forces. He said that there were several folks within the sound of his voice that God had already talked to about entering full time ministry as an evangelist, missionary or pastor. Johnny felt a tug on his heart that he was one of these folks being called into full time service.

That night before bed, Johnny wrestled with the idea of quitting his job, selling his 1st and only home and moving his family to who knows where.

It was a big step and not to be taken lightly. After all, he was now married and had two little ones. He needed more than a tug on his heartstrings to know that this was really God speaking to him.

So Johnny called out to God asking for a sign so he could know for sure that this was the next step on his way to glory. That same night, about midnight, when Johnny was fast asleep, he had a dream. It was in color and looked as if he was watching a video of things to come.

The dream or vision, Johnny wasn't sure which, showed a really big tornado approaching a certain city that had tall buildings with lots of glass windows. He could hear the explosions and even feel the wind blowing as the tornado ripped through the center of town.

He saw himself running with other people down a narrow street between glass walled buildings that were being torn apart just a few feet away. Then he saw himself at the top of one very tall building that had a panoramic view of the city with windows all around its top floor where he was standing. He saw many families crying in fear of their lives as the storm approached.

It was then that Johnny received his conformation from God about becoming a full time pastor. He saw himself preaching to the crowd and calling the folks to repentance and salvation. Then he fell fast asleep with no more dreams.

Now Johnny very rarely had a dream and when he did it was never in color and he never remember them. He just had bits and pieces that had no meaning. However, this dream was a full-length movie of the future with him playing the leading role. Plus, he was able to remember it all in detail, not just right after the dream but for many years.

A few days later the Lord explained the dream to Johnny as he prayed about it. The tornado was the judgment of God that was to come in the last days upon the wicked. The destruction was the crumbling of man's pride, ego, anti-God attitudes and rebellion. The part where Johnny was preaching just prior to the judgment of God was a picture of God's will for Johnny. It was also God's message of hope to the people of earth that it was not too late to get right with Him and follow Jesus while they still had breath.

Johnny was convinced and in the next night meeting surrendered his heart and life to full-time ministry. Yes, he sold his house, quit his job and enrolled in a Bible Institute using his GI Bill as a source of funding.

He was happy but no one else was. His wife refused to go with him. His mother said he must be mistaken. His pastor tried to redirect him into a 4-year college and his friends felt he was too long winded to be a preacher.

Again rejection raised its ugly head to stop the move of God in Johnny's life. But this time Johnny ignored all the naysayers. He knew that God had answered his plea for a sign and used it to fall back on when things got worse.

Johnny shared his dream with everyone that would listen but no one had the insight to see what God was doing. They discarded it as though it were a fable and looked at Johnny as though he was not all there. So Johnny shut his mouth and went on to do what he knew was right.

As Johnny prayed before the Lord, he was reminded of a scripture that came from the Old Testament. It said, is effect, that *God will make a way where there is no way*. It was then that he realized that God had to make a way for him and he needed to wait for it to appear. *(See gallery of poems… "The "Way Maker"" on page 78)*

Meanwhile, back on he home front, Johnny was faced with a rebellious wife that loved the things of the world more than she loved God. Thus came the arguments, hard feelings and so on.

Johnny finally gave up on his dream. However, God did not. He spoke to Johnny's wife and she said she didn't want to hinder God's work and she would go with him. Her submission was short lived because at the 1st sign of hardship she began an "I Told You So" critical campaign against him. They fought continually and she found fault with everyone around her.

Johnny had several invitations to minister and one was seriously looking at him as their next pastor. However, his marital life was in shambles and he walked away from being an eagle and again joined the chickens in he barnyard.

God's will was set aside because the price was too much to pay. The irony of it all was that Johnny's marital life still suffered and finally broke into little pieces ending in a divorce after ten long and frustrating years. His 1st wife turned into an alcoholic, developed a brain aneurysm and died several years later.

Johnny moved too fast out of loneliness and did not consult God. His 1st wife married him to escape an abusive father. Love never played a role in their marriage. It was a perfect example of living outside of God's perfect will.

CHAPTER SIX
A Gift From God

J OHNNY WAS LEFT WITH THE care of his two children while fighting his X-wife for custody and visitation rights. This went on until the kids were of legal age and continued until her death.

Johnny embraced the raising of his two children but was not all that educated in child rearing. He held the legal right of primary residency. He followed the path of least resistance but tried to instill Christian values in both of his kids. However, his x-wife's continual hatred twisted the minds of his children so much that they resisted his love and care. Over the years they both drifted off to do their own thing.

By now, Johnny was well acquainted with rejection and was not thrown for a loop over being rejected. He just kept on loving the kids and raised them the best he knew how. Trial and error played a big part in Johnny's methodology as long as it centered in love. *(See Gallery of poems… "Don't Worry" on page 70)*

Suddenly and without warning, God tossed a gift Johnny's way. It was a helpmeet, not a maid or a servant but a genuine beautiful woman to love and adore. They were married and the female perspective was added to Johnny's thinking process.

The kids had another adult to recon with and reject. But Johnny had a lover who was willing to love his children as her own. She was a gift from God wrapped in a perfect little package that was Sexy, *"New York Tough"* and most of all Loving.

This was a lady of class but also a lady not afraid to speak her mind and stand up for what she felt was right.

Johnny's 1st wife ran away from life. But this new gal was ready and willing to embrace it. She was indeed in pursuit of happiness. It was Johnny that carried all the baggage.

Johnny had been divorced going on three years when he hooked up with his "Fair Lady." He appeared to be healed and over any hang-ups from his 10-year marital ordeal.

However, once he said, "I Do" he slowly began to experience illusions of sorts. He knew that he was with his "Fair Lady" but it felt like he was once again trapped in a marital cell that would surely bring torment and grief.

He began to see his 1st wife all over again and feared the worst. He argued about many things when there was no basis for an argument. Johnny was a classic nut-job. He lost his lover and himself in a death spiral of fear and heartache.

However, the story didn't end in tragedy. There was no loss of life or 2nd divorce. God spoke again to Johnny's heart and calmed his emotional sea.

He said, *"Johnny! Take another look at your "Fair Lady" She is still with you and loves you. What you are feeling is a lie. Take another look."*

So Johnny looked again and again and again until he could see through the cloud of despair that hung over his soul. Every time he felt a flashback, he would let out a silent scream that called his feelings a lie and then he would say to himself, "This is my, "Fair Lady" in whom I give all my love and trust.

The baggage was strapped to Johnny's waist. It took a while for it to be dislodged but it happened. He finally found victory and was set free.

Johnny was now free to be with his, "Fair Lady" but his, "Fair Lady", was not there emotionally. She had been hurt from all the struggling and miscommunications that transpired during Johnny's illusive ordeal. Her "Where is my Johnny?" became Johnny's, "Where is my Fair Lady?" Johnny realized that he was the cause of his new wife's emotional suffering.

So Johnny set out to be her healing agent; to love her and cherish her and show her that he was not really that angry man she was living with. He was the man that his "Fair Lady" married. That other guy was not really Johnny. Over the ensuing years, he proved his personality to be the lover that his, "Fair Lady" married. The angry man died when Johnny came out of his illusions.

Slowly but surely, day after day, the arguments drifted away like a cloud blown in the wind. Love began to emerge and took its rightful place as their binding force.

What God meant for this couple was only good. Johnny finally found his soul mate. It took an act of God, lots of soul searching and continual prayer to bring back what was lost. Johnny dedicated himself to making changes, if necessary, to make life better. He changed jobs, attitudes, mannerisms and even his way of thinking. He no longer jumped into a dispute. Instead, he looked for the source that was behind it all and most of the time found an evil influence or a simple miscommunication.

Johnny prayed against misunderstandings, as did his "Fair lady."

Together, they kicked the devil out of the details and joined forces to resolve the issues at hand. Life was good again. Little Johnny Jones was now pushing 40-years old.

God sent both of them

"A Splash of Love"

Johnny loved his "Fair Lady" and she loved him. The splash of love that fell from the heavens baptized them both in the love of God. Oh what joy and comfort they found in the presence of the Lord. It was as if they were newlyweds all over again.

They possessed the greatest love of all and freely shared it with each other and anyone else that needed it. Yes, they encountered lots of rejection from various sources. Folks were jealous of their romance and angry with them for speaking of their love. But Johnny still pressed on in the midst of adversity and found that God had prepared a table for him in the presence of his enemies.

So Johnny enjoyed the blessings and laughed at his enemies.

CHAPTER SEVEN
Religious Fury

R ELIGION NEVER TOOK OVER JOHNNY'S life even though he was all caught up in its fury. In fact, there was a time when Johnny left the organized church for a small house fellowship. He was the number one critic of religion and often commented on how many churches were creating false Christians. He had difficulty balancing what the scripture said about salvation with the lifestyles of those who professed a belief in Christ.

On the one hand, he saw salvation as a free gift from God that is received and held dear to one's heart. But on the other hand he saw religion, telling folks that the only way to God was through good works i.e. by obeying the laws of God. Some even believed that if a person died with unconfessed sin that he or she would not enter God's pearly gates.

Then there was the "Repent! Or die" teachings that were harsh but scriptural. The Bible did say, "Without repentance there is no salvation." (Acts 3:19)

Religion softened the plea by telling the lost that all they had to do was accept Jesus and everything would be ok. Repentance was never taught or even presented as a qualifier. Thus many joined the church as though it were a moral social club where they could escape the guilt of past sins. There was even a movement that said their religion was the one true religion.

Johnny believed in "Repentance" but, like most other followers, had no idea what to repent of. Once he went through the list of past blunders and rebellious actions, he became frustrated with the daily routine of "I am sorry for"…Blah! Blah! Blah! The repetition drove him crazy and eventually became meaningless. He was never sure if he forgot a sin to confess or not.

So Johnny sought the Lord for a resolution to his dilemma. As he prayed and read his Bible, he saw what was written in Romans about all had come short of the glory of God and all were sinners. He also read where Adam's original sin of rebellion brought death to him and passed on to all of his descendants.

He quickly realized that he was not a sinner because he sinned along life's way but rather sinned because he was a sinner at heart. He had a death sentence on his head and was marked for eternal punishment because he fell short of God's glory, which was put into man at his creation and lost by Adam's transgression. He was born a sinner. It was in his DNA. He, like everyone else, had a nature that was sinful and always missed the mark of God's righteousness.

Johnny realized that his stubborn nature, argumentative attitudes and anger were a result of his fallen nature. Instead of walking in God's glory all the day long, Johnny walked in his own selfishness and demonstrated pride, jealousy, hatred, and a host of other evil attributes.

His repentance found a new meaning. He stopped repenting for things he did wrong and cried out to God in repentance for who he was deep down, a sinful soul in need of a savior. He realized that he had no power in himself to attain godliness.

Johnny journeyed among many different theological beliefs and church doctrines that were clearly unscriptural. He was no final authority but did have enough common sense to see that what was being taught did not match up with Biblical truth.

So Johnny again suffered rejection but this time it was from other churchgoers. By this time, Johnny was not afraid to speak up and often did. However, sometimes his, "Fair Lady," would beat him to the punch and challenge the Bible study leader or even the pastor. She was equally versed in matters of God's word, faith and Biblical truth.

Way back in Johnny's past there was a little old lady that helped him come to the truth. She was the spitting image of an 18th century grandmother with her silver hair in a bun and even black laced up shoes. She was 85-years old when he met her. She ran a small Bible study in her home that was not connected to any organized religion. She just followed the leading of the Lord and taught the Word of God to young Christians.

This little old lady ran a home Bible study in another state for 20-years until the Lord told her to pack up and move…and so she did, all alone at age 75 she mover across the United States to an unfamiliar city where she spent 10 years sharing God's Word with whoever dropped in.

Then she responded to a call from the gal who took over her 1st Bible study to come back and resume the leadership of that class due to her failing health. So she went back and took over where she left off 10-years before.

Johnny's beloved Bible confidant left him alone to seek out a new mother in the Lord. Instead, Johnny was led to a little church that seemed to have the love and power of God. He came back to the fellowship of the church and fell under the leadership of a dedicated man of God who took over where his little old lady left off.

Johnny still had a hard time seeing himself as an eagle until he entered Bible College. He had always been a below average student but that was not due to being stupid. It was because of his fear of rejection and inability to soar like an eagle. It was easier to be a chicken in the barnyard, unnoticed and hidden in the shadows.

The day of reckoning came when Johnny received his tests back from several teachers. They all had A's or B's written on them. Johnny was not a good student but God made him one. His ability to learn and recall what he read had blossomed like a fragile flower before the Lord. *(See gallery of poems… "Fragile Flower Red" on page 87)*

Johnny started being recognized by his fellow students. It was then that little Johnny Jones realized he was indeed an eagle. He also realized that he didn't need the praises of men to go on with God. All he needed was God and God had never left his side. He was there working everything together for good because Johnny loved God and was called according to His purposes.

CHAPTER EIGHT
The Business of Living Life

LITTLE JOHNNY JONES IS ALL grown up now. He has raised a family, spent a fortune moving around the country in search of a good job and was able to discover his true identity; that it comes from a relationship with Jesus. It's been a trip but his "Fair Lady" has been at his side every day and the Holy Spirit has led them most of the time. *(See gallery of poems... "The Lord's Little Two By Four" on page 73)*

God's blessings, over the years, overwhelmed them. God sent support during times of unemployment; jobs when the economy was in a decline; love amidst rejection; and even Divine revelation when Johnny needed discernment and wisdom.

These things were more precious to Johnny than silver and gold because they brought peace of mind and comfort to his heart.

Johnny was no different than other dedicated Christians. He and his "Fair Lady" served the Lord in many unusual ways, like using poetry to minister; writing and producing one act plays. Also through big websites that drew thousands of visitors every year; through automatic dialing to area residents by phone with a special salvation message and most of all being open to the voice of the Spirit to share Jesus with others.

Johnny tied his hand at being a pastor of a small congregation. He started a church from nothing in one city, became a youth minister in another and was a teacher of evangelism to folks that participated in Wednesday night visitation for his church.

Finally, after lots of soul searching, Johnny read in the Bible that Paul was not only a minister of the good news of Jesus but was also a tent maker, meaning Prayer Shawls). He did not rely on the people that he taught to feed him. They could not control him with their influence or money. He was his own man and that's what Johnny liked.

So Johnny decided not to chase after a paid position in the church. Instead he became a tent maker of sorts. He went back to the sales arena where he did well before and earned a living while at the same time preaching and teaching as the Lord provided opportunities. He even became an author, writing Christian fiction and "How-To" books.

Johnny supported foreign missions, the smuggling of Bibles behind the "Iron" curtain and looked for ways to be a blessing in his community.

The business of living life was full of activity, most of which was at the leading of the Holy Spirit. Sickness and sorrow were banished from Johnny's house.

Even arguments dropped to an all time low. Johnny and his, "Fair Lady" saw a scripture that said they were not to let the sun do down upon their wrath so they made it a policy to stay up all night, if necessary, until love once again filled their hearts and home.

CHAPTER NINE
Walking In The Clouds

Little Johnny Jones started his walk in the clouds in a small country church. His mother chased him and his siblings off to Sunday school every Sunday. She worked six days a week and found Sunday mornings to be perfect as a quiet time to read the newspaper and have an extended cup of coffee.

Sunday school and children's church gave her almost two and a half hours of, "Me Time" where she could relax and prepare the Sunday meal without being interrupted.

Johnny would leave early to walk the ¼ of a mile down the old country road and across the wooden bridge so he could play with the other kids outside the brick church until the teacher called them inside.

Johnny liked church but did not see it as a place of worship and learning where he could draw close to his creator. It was a social gathering place for fun with the neighborhood kids.

Johnny's dad was Catholic and never went to church. Mom was not really involved with spiritual matters at that time. The family was Protestant like most others in the area.

Johnny joined the Royal Ambassadors, a youth group of sorts where he and others would meet on Wednesday nights. It was there that Johnny was introduced to the idea of memorizing Bible verses. Little did he know that he was laying a foundation for life as he memorized scriptures.

Johnny was hiding the Word of God in his heart that he might not sin against God. He did not see this memory thing as a law to be kept but rather an exercise in showing off.

Johnny learned John 3:16, John 3:3 and John 6:33; then Romans 5:12 and 8:28-30 and many others. He became good at reciting Bible verses but found out very quickly that when he recited them, most people had an adverse reaction.

The verses were anointed for they were the living Word of God. When read or recited they often made folks uncomfortable. That's because the scriptures dealt with man as a sinner in need of salvation. They brought conviction to the soul and a call to repent.

Now Johnny didn't understand all of what he was reciting. He just saw rejection in their eyes and patronization coming from their lips. He never thought to listen to the meaning of the verses he quoted.

After moving to Florida, Johnny lost interest in church. He was growing up and found girls to be more interesting. Although he liked them he had no idea what to do with them. It was like fishing for a shark but afraid of really catching one. If he did, he'd be taking the risk of getting bit while reeling it in.

One day, in the 7th grade, Johnny caught a shark and was planning to take her to the 7th grade dance. The possibility of getting bit was so great that Johnny backed out at the last moment. He later got over the fear of girls and dated in high school.

Church life gave way to teenage hormones and attitudes. Johnny became a skirt chaser. He also chased jeans, shorts and jogging outfits, as long as a girl was wearing them.

Johnny also fell into gambling. It wasn't big time but it was regular nickel and dime games where a guy could lose $20 in one pot. Thus went Johnny's hard earned money and he was often disabled financially and couldn't date.

Johnny found the perfect remedy for his gambling losses. He stopped gambling. His female interests were more important.

Johnny's walk through the clouds was short lived but was sure to emerge again as he entered adulthood.

There would be many jobs, military service in the USN, twice married, kids, college, several job losses, family deaths and more… but through it all Johnny kept on keeping on using his love for God and Biblical promises as hooks to hang his faith on.

Little Johnny Jones found his place in the clouds. He is now on cloud nine resting in the glory of the Lord. He is blessed beyond measure and full of peace and joy because he is walking in the Spirit of the living God who loves him and remains at his side. Even the Angel of The Lord sets up his camp around Johnny because Johnny reverences God. They are there to deliver him from life's many temptations and trials.

CHAPTER TEN
The Best And Worst of Times

You'll never guess what happened to little Johnny Jones on his way to Glory. We'll start with some of the worst times in his life.

1. He had a brain hemorrhage when he was a baby and wasn't expected to live through the night.

2. He married a girl he didn't love and lived 10-years in a life of heartache.

3. His father died and he didn't have a chance to say goodbye.

4. He was in a car accident on his 18th birthday and the 1st police officer on the scene was his dad.

5. He lost his high paying job and spent almost a year unemployed.

6. His son had scarlet fever and almost died.

7. He experienced illusions from his 1st marriage and feared that his 2nd marriage would be the same.

There were many good things that came Johnny's way that re-established his selfworth and confidence. Here are a few best times in Johnny's life.

1. When he was, "Born Again," and filled with the Holy Spirit of God.

2. When he met his second wife and married for love.

3. When he received a special gifting from the Lord to write. Now he is an author of several books.

4. When he actually met Jesus in a spiritual encounter where Jesus saved him from a backslidden condition.

5. When his mom went beyond the age of 98.

6. When he retired from working full time.

7. When he received "A Splash of Love" from God that continues even unto this day.

The list of worst times and best times in Johnny's life can go on for many pages but time does not allow for more here.

Johnny Jones is not much different that most red-blooded American men. He loves his country, is law-abiding, votes in every election, is conservative, respects the national flag, believes in the 2nd amendment, trusts in God, prays for a better tomorrow and loves his wife.

Johnny had some "Worst of Times" occurrences but he also had many more "Best of Times" experiences. One of the very best was falling in love with his," Fair Lady"

Johnny had been pretty much out of it after his 1st divorce. It was three years later when God brought him a soul mate. It all happened like this…

Johnny was an executive. He was the boss and responsible for hiring and firing among other things. He needed a secretary and advertised for one. The end result of the interview process was two equally qualified candidates. One was married and one was not.

During the interview with the single woman, Johnny noticed that she was from New York and was of Italian descent. Plus she was shapely, very attractive and friendly. He asked her to pull up her chair closed to his desk so they could talk more freely. However, the real reason was due to his poor eyesight.

Johnny was also from New York and loved the way this woman talked. You could tell right away that she was a New Yorker. She made him feel right at home. (Johnny loved New Yorkers but he grew up in Virginia.)

Johnny looked over her file and saw on the application that she successfully typed 100 words per minute. The position involved mostly typing. However, as they made small talk, Johnny shifted from a business interview to a general discussion.

He couldn't decide whether he wanted to date her or hire her. One of his interview questions was: *Do you make good Lasagna?*

Well Johnny had a hard time deciding so he tossed both files on the desk of his office manager and said, *"Both are qualified, pick one."* And that's how his "Fair Lady" became part of the team.

A few months later, three female employees resigned and walked out as a protest to Johnny's management style. He was vindicated of any wrong doing and preceded to hire more staff. In that process, he promoted the New Yorker to office manager.

Six months later, after working together every day, Johnny asked the New Yorker to be his, "Fair Lady." The next day the New Yorker said she would.

Their courtship was during work and special events that Johnny headed up for his company. Once married, Johnny had to fire his beloved wife. It was all because of a nepotism clause in the employee manual that he wrote the previous year.

Then Johnny heard from the Lord about his, "Fair Lady." God was glad and even inspired her employment. However, the Lord was more concerned about Johnny's walk with Him. He told Johnny in an, "I Know That I Know" unction that he could not have his current job and his newfound love. He would have to accept one and let the other fall by the wayside.

The job was too political and demanding and his "Fair Lady" was unaccustomed to politics, head games and power struggles.

So Johnny gave up his job for his, "Fair Lady" which brought on the worst time ever. It was of God. It was the right thing to do. But it was hard to swallow as it took almost a year to secure another comparable position. Unemployment took its toll.

Every time Johnny looks back on those days he gives thanks to the Lord because he made the right decision to keep love alive in his heart and to fulfill the prayers of his lover.

CHAPTER ELEVEN
Crazy Stunts By Design

Tree Topping

JOHNNY DID SOME CRAZY STUNTS during his childhood days. One stunt was to climb a skinny pine tree all the way to the top and then let his friends on the ground chop in down with hatchet. Riding the tree down was a real thrill to a 10-year old boy especially when he had to jump off just before the tree hit the ground. Johnny called it, "Tree Topping." All the kids did it and it was fun.

Mice Hunting

Another fun crazy stunt was to hunt field mice with a bow and arrow. Hitting one was really hard but shooting and retrieving arrows passed the time on a summer afternoon. Johnny did hit one and it squirmed on his arrow and bled all over the place, so much so, that Johnny never did that stunt again. The fun was shooting at something that moved. Hitting it was too sad to continue.

Dirt Clod Fighting

Most of the boys in the neighborhood had Daisy Air Rifles. Johnny did too. It had a kick to it when you pulled the trigger and was perfect for a dirt clod fight. All you had to do was push the barrel of your rifle into the dirt until it filled up about one inch. Then you aim at the enemy and fire. A clod of dirt would fly out of the barrel and hit the opposing team. That is, if they were close enough.

Frogs & Snake Hunting

Johnny sometimes went with other kids walking along the banks of the Swamp Road Creek in the late afternoon. They all took three pronged gig polls so they could gig their prey. Some of the kids actually gigged frogs but Johnny didn't like too. He had fun pretending to be tough but always missed. Most of his time was watching out for water moccasins, also known as cottonmouth snakes. *(It's a venomous pit viper snake species found in southeastern parts of the United States.)*

Creek Splashing

Johnny and some of the other kids tied a rope to a branch high up in a tree that was very close to the creek. Then they would grab hold of the rope and run towards the creek. The rope was long and allowed the swinger to swing over the creek where he or she would let go and splash into the creek. It was lots of fun. However, one kid had to act as lookout to warn everybody of danger because there were snakes and snapping turtles in the creek.

Swimming With The Turds

One of the craziest stunts was to go swimming in the lake that the Navy used for its filtering of solid waste. Johnny had a real rubber life raft. He and some other boys would use it in the lake and paddle along through an occasional turd floating in the water. One day, the boys saw no turds so they jumped into the water for a quick swim. However, they quickly got back into the raft because they saw turds everywhere. Their quick swim was through the turds.

The Navy Bullet Hunt

Johnny lived less that a mile from a Navy Jet Base that had a shooting range. He and some other boys would sneak onto the base by following the railroad tracks until they were behind the gun range. Then it was clear sailing to the place where all the bullets were that were shot from guns and rifles. They had a bag and picked up all sizes of bullets, never realizing that the range might be occupied when they were there. Fortunately, Johnny's dad saw the bullets, questioned how he got them and forbid him to ever go there again.

Fishing Pier Jumping

Johnny loved to fish and often went to the fishing pier. One year a hurricane swept the end of the pier out to sea leaving a rickety structure to be battered by the incoming tide. Johnny and friends loved to break through the Danger! Sign at the entrance and walk to the end of what was left of the pier. Then they would, one by one, jump into the ocean, a 15-foot drop as they let out a yell. Of course the cops were called and they came after the boys but they jumped again to their freedom and swam away.

Night Pool Hopping

Another crazy stunt was to go pool hopping at night. Here's how it worked. One guy would stay in the driver's seat with the engine running. Three other guys would run and jump into a hotel's pool as they screamed and laughed. Then back to the car that sped away to the next hotel. It was fun until they got caught.

CHAPTER TWELVE
Believe It Or Not

JOHNNY HAD SOME, *"BELIEVE IT or Not"* experiences while on his way to glory. He is hoping to have more as he moves through his twilight years.

The rainbow experience was especially interesting. Yes, Johnny was at the end of the rainbow. He actually was there.

It all happened when Johnny and his young son were in his car. Johnny was driving down the road heading home from the store. It had just rained and the sky was still somewhat gray. Suddenly there appeared a giant rainbow in the sky. One end was over land and the other in the lane where Johnny was driving.

The rainbow was like no other he had seen. It was full of colors, bright and stretched for miles over land. The end that touched the pavement was gloriously arrayed with color.

As Johnny approached the bow, he saw that he was going right into the center of the colors. They appeared on his vehicle and still stayed bold in color. Then they rippled as he passed through them, first on the hood, then the windshield and finally the trunk. *(See gallery of poems… "Chasing Rainbows" on page 68)*

Johnny passed right through the rainbow. It was a beautiful sight. As he entered and while in the bow, gold pieces of eight fell from the sky. He quickly pulled over and gathered them up, fighting with other drivers for the pot of gold.

All in all, Johnny kicked some butt, gathered over 60 gold coins and drove away three feet taller.

Believe It or Not

There was another time that Johnny met himself when renewing his driver's license. Yea, it was weird. He was downtown on the last day of his birth month and needed to renew his driver's license. He went into the location, took the eye test, had his picture taken and sat down as instructed until his license was ready.

The lady called his name and he left his seat and went to the window. However, he was not the only Johnny Jones at the window. There was another that was ten years younger standing there too.

Johnny thought to himself, what are the odds of two men showing up to renew their driver's licenses on the very last day with the same name and birthday?

The younger Johnny Jones kept looking at the older Johnny Jones and finally said, "So you are what I'll look like ten years from now? Johnny laughed and said, "Yep"

The younger Johnny didn't believe the older Johnny that they had the same name and birth date. He demanded that Johnny show him some identification. Johnny just laughed and said, "It's being processed, stick around."

Johnny was amazed that he had an almost look-a- like in the same city. They had different mothers together; they went to different schools together; they married different wives together and yet never ran into each other before.

Believer It or Not

Johnny loved to go swimming as a kid. He often went out in the ocean after fish with a spear gun. He'd snorkel and dive down to the reefs looking to spear fish. When he speared one, he'd toss it into a basket that had an anchor attached so it wouldn't drift away.

One day, a shark, smelling the blood in the water, came by to investigate. Johnny had to be a quarter of a mile off shore. It was a long swim back to a place of safety.

Well the shark was about six feet long with a mouth full of teeth. It was scary. Suddenly the shark began to circle the basket and Johnny in a wide oval. Then it would narrow the circle closing in.

Johnny started to swim, dragging the basket with him. His destination was the shoreline. As Johnny dangled in the ocean, kicking and swimming feverishly, the shark moved closer and closer. It came dangerously close to Johnny several times.

Johnny pointed his spear gun at the shark poking at it and trying to keep it at bay. But that action didn't seem to work because the shark attacked the basket striking it with its snout and trying to pull it apart with its teeth.

Johnny was too far from shore to get help. It was up to him to save himself and his catch. He aimed at the shark and shot his spear gun. The spear penetrated the back area of the shark near its tail fin.

The spear was attached to a heavy nylon cord that was also attached to Johnny's spear gun. He pulled on the cord to release the spear but it had entered the shark too deeply and would not come out.

The shark then began to swim away dragging Johnny and his basket with him. Johnny would not cut the cord or drop his gun. It was a shark tug-of- war for a while as the shark pulled Johnny out to sea.

It was a lucky day for Johnny that the Coastguard was conducting rescue exercises about five miles off shore. They saw Johnny and his basket breaking the waves as the shark swam towards them.

The Coastguard rescued Johnny by cutting the cord and brought him onboard. He got a hot meal on the Coastguard Cutter, was refreshed and had a free ride in the rubber rescue boat back to the shore.

Believe It Or Not

Johnny dated a lot in his early twenties. One of his more memorable dates was with a queen. She was the Florida Citrus Queen. She came to his town as part of a promotional tour. Johnny was invited to a gathering, met her and asked her out for a night on the town. He and she were not married at the time.

Johnny showed her such a great time that the Mayor of his town received a letter a few weeks later protesting Johnny's actions and treatment of their Queen. All they did was go dancing and had a good time but that was taboo for their Queen. The Citrus commission never accepted an invitation again to come to any event in Johnny's town.

Johnny felt good about being such a gentlemen even though he was criticized.

Believe It Or Not

Johnny is a minister of the good news. If you are wondering what the, "Good News" is, read John 3:16.

The good news is that God sent His only Son to earth from heaven to die a cruel death on a Roman cross at a place called Calvary. His sacrifice was the penalty for everyone's sin. He did this because he loved mankind and wanted to bring back what was lost, i.e. His image and likeness in man.

God's call was very simple, repent and believe on Jesus. He would be to door through which man could see the kingdom of God and have eternal life.

Little Johnny Jones became a preacher and even now proclaims this gospel (Good News) everywhere to everyone who will listen.

He and his "Fair Lady" experienced (A Splash of love) from God.

Believe It Or Not

CHAPTER THIRTEEN
A Time To Cry

THERE WERE MANY HAPPY TIMES in Johnny's life but there were also times to cry and Johnny did. He, like most men, went through times of sorrow and suffered the agony of the moment. They took a toll on his emotions.

One such time was when he left London Bridge, Virginia. for parts unknown. He knew he would wind up somewhere in Florida but was still afraid of the unknown. He was old enough to restrain his tears but cried inside for weeks.

The kids in Florida were different. Their accents were not like his. They were not acceptant of new kids. They enjoyed getting a laugh by criticizing others. It was a terrible place and there was no way of escape. He had to adjust but the kids around him were mean and would not let up on him.

Johnny finally worked through all the issues and went on to better things. He even found a girlfriend along the way.

Another such time was when Johnny's father died. They were never real close but close enough that Johnny felt the loss. His personality developed after the similitude of his dad. His humor, his perspectives in life, his moral compass and his common sense all came from his dad.

Johnny really suffered the loss of his dad because he was not there to say goodbye before he passed away. He wanted so bad to tell his father that he loved him but it never happened. Johnny shed a tear or two or three at his dad's funeral and still misses him after more than 26-years.

Johnny also cried when he fell out of favor with his family. It's been over 15 years ago that his son married a Brazilian divorcee who snatched him away from his friends and family. It's been longer that his older sister left her husband to live with another woman. It's been over ten years that his daughter dropped out of sight and does not want to communicate. Johnny stood up for what was right and lost everything. There was a price to pay for being moral and he paid it.

Finally, Johnny cried when his, "Fair Lady," was rushed to the emergency room during the worldwide Covid-19 Pandemic. She was delirious and on the verge of a diabetic coma. She pulled through after a week in the ICU and another in rehab. She is now on the road to recovery. Johnny's prayers and the prayers of many others brought her from a very critical ketoacidosis patient to being almost normal again.

There is a time to laugh and a time to cry. There is a time to rejoice and a time to be sad. These are the times that made Johnny cry. It is good that he felt and expressed his emotions. It means he is alive and human.

Johnny cried before the Lord and He cleansed his soul of the grief and disappointments. He is a better man because of it. *(See gallery of poems... "Angels Cry "Holy"" on page 81)*

CHAPTER FOURTEEN
Tomorrow And Beyond

JOHNNY HAS A PARTICULAR MINDSET. He lives in the moment, plans for the future and discards all the evil and regret from the past. He believes it is not good for a person to worry about life and what may or may not happen. (*See gallery of poems… "Don't Worry" on page 70*)

Johnny believes that when you follow God, you flow with His Spirit and soar like the eagle above life's trials and tribulations. It all happens by faith, knowing that you are in the care of a loving creator.

Johnny knows that it rains on the just and the unjust. He understands that he is not exempt from temptation, selfish desires, rejection, and even attacks from evil forces. He knows all of this but he also knows that the Lord said He would be with His children until the very end of the age. He will never forsake them. Johnny's God is greater than anything that comes his way.

Here's some of the things that Johnny believes are yet to come and await mankind just around the corner.

1. ***The days of Noah will return***…they were eating, drinking and marring right up to the day of the flood. It took them totally by surprise even though Noah built an ark in their midst and preached destruction to anyone who would listen.

So shall it be when Jesus returns. He will come like a thief in the night, totally unexpected and take them all away.

2. ***Thing will progressively get worse leading up to the end of the age.*** The earth cannot escape God's judgment. It will surely happen.

The wicked will suffer God's wrath. Death and destruction will befall mankind because of their rejection of God and His only begotten Son, Jesus.

3. ***The Antichrist will arise***…in political and religious life and deceive many, saying that he is God. He will even perform miracles.

This individual is evil and will set the world in motion for the final death of the human race as we know it.

4. ***Many will realize the truth of God's word and come to Jesus***. They will not be "The Wicked" that seek power and self-gratification but rather those that really didn't understand. Their eyes will be opened and they will repent.

5. ***Johnny and his, "Fair Lady" will ride off into the sunset of life***, enjoying the beauty of the Lord, the blessings of a relationship with Jesus and the anointing of the Holy Spirit.

6. ***Johnny will author other books of Christian Fiction, Romance, Faith***.

CHAPTER FIFTEEN
The "Whosoever" Scenario

A CERTAIN MAN ASKED A LITTLE boy once, "What do you want to be when you grow up" The little boy thought for a few moments and then replied. He said, "Sir? I would like to be a "Whosoever."

The man laughed and said, "A Whosoever, what is that?" The little boy again replied saying, "Don't you read your Bible?" The little boy was Johnny Jones.

Johnny continued to explain. "If I become a doctor or lawyer or a successful business man, I no doubt will gain wealth, fame and maybe even power over others but if I lose my own soul in the process, what has it benefited me?"

"On the other hand, if I become a "whosoever" I gain eternal life. I will be blessed in this life and the one to come"

Johnny was wise beyond his years. He was an avid reader of the Bible and loved to learn about God. His desire to know led him to the greatest discovery of all times, the meaning of life and eternity. It was all there, wrapped up in one word spoken by Jesus, **"Whosoever."**

So, the word, "Whosoever," describes an unknown person that does something. It requires action on the part of the unknown individual. He or she must do something in order to be a, "Whosoever."

Whosoever or whoever, whichever you like, must do something… jump off a cliff or get in the car or follow the leader…(*there is always a reward. It can be in blessings or punishment based upon the action taken by* "The Whosoever.")

Let's look at some "Whosoever" scriptures to see the actions of a, "Whosoever," type of person.

"For whosoever *shall call* upon the name of the Lord shall be saved." *Romans 10:13*

"For God so loved the world, that he gave his only begotten Son, that whosoever *believeth* in him should not perish, but have everlasting life." *John 3:16*

The actions of the, "Whosoever", is clear. It is to call upon the name of the Lord and to believe in Him. There is no mention of joining a church, following a certain religion, keeping a strict set of rules, or doing lots of good deeds.

Salvation, per John 3:16, is offered to all who believe. It is a free gift given by God out of a deep love for us, even though we are full of sin. Listen to what the Bible says.

- "And you, being dead in your sins and the uncircumcision of your flesh, hath he quickened together with him, having forgiven you all trespasses; Blotting out the handwriting of ordinances that was against us, which was contrary to us, and took it out of the way, nailing it to his cross" *Colossians 2:13-14*

- "As for you, you were dead in your transgressions and sins, in which you used to live when you followed the ways of this world and of the ruler of the kingdom of the air, the spirit who is now at work in those who are disobedient."

- "All of us also lived among them at one time, gratifying the cravings of our flesh and following its desires and thoughts. Like the rest, we were by nature deserving of wrath.

- But because of his great love for us, God, who is rich in mercy, made us alive with Christ even when we were dead in transgressions—it is by grace you have been saved.

- And God raised us up with Christ and seated us with him in the heavenly realms in Christ Jesus, in order that in the coming ages he might show the incomparable riches of his grace, expressed in his kindness to us in Christ Jesus." (Colossians 2:13)

- "For it is by grace you have been saved, through faith—and this is not from yourselves, it is the gift of God—not by works, so that no one can boast. For we are God's handiwork, created in Christ Jesus to do good works, which God prepared in advance for us to do."
Ephesians 2:1-10 NIV

Johnny told the man that salvation is by the grace of God. It is offered to the, "Whosoevers" of this world. They are those that accept the offer. If the call to salvation is rejected, the one who rejects it is not a, "Whosoever" and thus misses out on its blessings.

Johnny open his Bible and shared other references where the word, "Whosoever" was used. There are some of them.

"Whosoever believes that Jesus is the Christ is born of God: and every one that loves him that begat loves him also that is begotten of him." **I John 5:1**

Then Jesus declared, "I am the bread of life. Whosoever comes to me will never go hungry, and whosoever believes in me will never be thirsty." **John 6:35**

"Therefore whosoever hears these sayings of mine, and does them, I will liken him unto a wise man, which built his house upon a rock." **Matthew 7:24**

"Whoever pursues righteousness and love finds life, prosperity and honor." **Proverbs 21:21**

"For whosoever shall be ashamed of me and of my words, of him shall the Son of man be ashamed, when he shall come in his own glory, and *in his* Father's, and of the holy angels." **Luke 9:26**

Then Johnny said to the man, "I am one of the, "Whosoevers" of my generation. I will proudly proclaim Jesus as Lord and Savior. I will not care if someone disagrees with me. I will follow Jesus anyway and share my faith with all who will listen."

"For God so loved the world, that he gave his only begotten Son, that whosoever *believeth* in him should not perish, but have everlasting life." *John 3:16*

Johnny made sure that the man understood that Jesus didn't say that God was angry or mad. He said that the call to salvation was a, "Splash of Love", from the heart of God. He also said that those who respond would not perish but instead attain eternal life.

A Note From the Author

The, "Whosoever" doctrine is an open invitation to all but limited to the few that accept it. The offer is to everyone but sadly, not everyone will believe.

Those that do believe attain the blessings. Those that do not are like the man that built his house without an adequate foundation. It fell into ruin when the storms of life came. Salvation is open to all and reserved for those who accept it.

So, the, "Whosoever" is one who, of his or her own free will, makes a choice to believe in Christ as Lord and Savior and follows His teachings.

You can be a, "Whosoever" and join millions of others through the ages that have been, "Born Again" into the family of God. It's a simple decision that is made by faith. We accept it by faith and we live it out by faith.

CONCLUSION

Little Johnny Jones started out as a well-adjusted 10-year old but he lost himself along life's way. He fought the age-old enemy, the King of Rejection. The ruthless Prince of Low Self-Worth enslaved him. He battled the armies of Insecurity and Intimidation.

However, God never left his side even when Johnny gave up and tried to be a chicken in the barnyard. He was, "Born Again", as an eagle and finally realized it. He took flight on the wings of the morning and soared into the sunset as his creator told him to do. *(See gallery of poems... "With Eagle's Wings" on page 89)*

Johnny is alive and well on planet earth. He is doing what he feels is God's will and is blessed to be able to walk with the Lord and his, "Fair Lady" in these last days.

GALLERY OF POEMS

The Little Chicken

A story for you
And a story for me.
This is the story
Of a little chicken
Who once sat on my knee.
With his feathers ruffled
And his eyes so bright,
The little chicken soared
In the midst of flight.
Around the barn
And beyond the tree,
Flew that little chicken
Back to my knee.
A bond of love
So true you see,
Between the little chicken
And me.
I watched him grow
And splash and play.
It seemed that the little chicken
Was here to stay.
But then one day
When I came home from play,
My little chicken
Wasn't there that day.
I sought and searched
And looked to see,
What had happened
To the little chicken
That once sat on my knee?
With a sadden heart

And tears in my eyes,
I came to the supper table
To find a surprise.
There in my plate
I learned of the fate
Of the little chicken
Who we all ate.

Poem By
John Marinelli
(A True Story)

Chasing Rainbows

Let's chase a rainbow
As it bows in the sky.
We'll get up real close
Just to wonder why.
We'll jump in the car
And zip down the street,
Hoping to find the place
Where the ground
And rainbow meet.

***

Closer and closer we move
To the end of the bow,
For it's touching the road
Where we're sure to go.
Suddenly! Like a flash
We'll pass through its glow,
And watch it shine
on the bumper,
then the hood
And over the window.
Then we'll dash away,
Always and forever to know
That once upon a time
We were at the end
of the Rainbow

Poem By
John Marinelli

All Creation Waits

A blue-gray sky
Winks at the dawn,
As the morning light
Sings its glorious song.
Life is flourishing everywhere,
Unaware of what's in store.
The sounds of spring beckons,
In a silent and peaceful roar.
Time marches onward,
Towards the brink of day,
As all of creation waits
For God's children to pray.

Poem By
John Marinelli

Don't Worry

Don't worry about tomorrow.
You did that yesterday.
Go on with your life
And remember always to pray.
Ask and it shall be given to you,
But this great truth you already know.
Rejoice and be happy, why? Because…
Your harvest comes from what you sow.
I will say it again and even more,
Until it becomes very very clear.
Tomorrow will take care of itself,
But worry is another word for fear.
Now here's what I want you to do.
Trust in the Lord and be of good cheer.
Drop the worry from your vocabulary
And cast out that demon of fear.

Poem By
John Marinelli

Arm's Length

I hold the world at arm's length,
That its choices do not interfere.
While it does its own thing,
I watch and wait over here.
My steps must not go that way,
For it's not where I need to be.
The Lord has shown me the path,
That will lead me to my destiny.
The call to stray is strong
And pulls at me now and then.
But I know that way
Is full of sorrow and sin.
I must move on in life
Beyond their beckoning call.
It's the right thing to do,
So I do not stumble or fall.
I will not be swayed or misled
By family, friends or business deal.
Their secret thoughts are not mine,
To consider, to admire or feel.
So I keep the world at "Arm's Length"
As I journey through this life.
My faith in Jesus keeps me strong,
As I walk in His glorious light.

Poem By
John Marinelli

Clutter

Clutter keeps the mind confused,
As images dance through the night.
Lost among those unimportant thoughts,
Are the dreams that once shined bright.
An endless parade of fear and doubt,
Crowds the mind to destroy our day.
Ever soaring on the wings of the soul,
Until it has formed an evil array.
But clutter is by one's choice,
Of those who dance to its beat.
Better to face imaginations' due
Than to fall into utter defeat.

Poem By
John Marinelli

The Lord's Little Two By Four

God has a little 2' X 4'
That rest on heaven's windowsill.
He uses it now and then,
When we stray from His will.
Sometimes we need a good "Bap";
With the Lord's little 2' X 4'
To knock out the confusion,
And help us to desire Him more.
The Lord's little 2' X 4'
Is what we sometimes need,
To get our thinking straight,
And keep our focus indeed.
The Lord's little 2' X 4'
Is fashioned from life's every trial,
So we do not stray from His will,
Or fall into an ungodly lifestyle.

Poem By
John Marinelli

I Find Myself In God

I find myself in God.
He is my, "Everything"
I know that He is Lord,
My Life, my Hope, and King.
I find myself in God,
Not the ways of sin.
Nor do I look to others,
To know who I really am.
I find myself in God,
To whom I bow on bended knee.
He alone is my joy and strength
And where I want to be.

Poem By
John Marinelli

"I AM" There

"I AM" There,
At the end of your broken dreams,
Before the sun rises over your day,
Prior to those tear-filled streams.
"I AM" There,
Down that road of despair,
When all appears to be lost,
And no one seems to care.
"I AM" There,
Over all of life's twists and turns,
When tomorrow is all but gone,
And when you are full of concerns.
"I AM" There,
Sayeth the Lord of Host,
To bring you hope and peace,
And the power of My Holy Ghost.
"I AM" There,
To be sure you make it through,
In the midst of every trial,
To bless your life and deliver you.
"I AM" There

Poem By
John Marinelli

The Pastor & The Master

If the pastor doesn't follow the Master,
Then I cannot follow the pastor.
But if the pastor walks with the Master,
Then I can walk with the pastor.

When pastors stray from the Master,
The sheep will stray from the pastor.
But when the pastor loves the Master,
God blesses the sheep and the pastor.
Jesus is the pastor's Master,
And why the sheep follow the Master.
For He is Lord over the pastor.
That's why they call Him Master.

The pastor and the Master--
The Master and the pastor--
The sheep follow the pastor
When the pastor follows the Master.

Poem By
John Marinelli

The Lighthouse

A lighthouse is a blessing,
To the ships that toss in the sea.
For it shows them the way,
Until they can clearly see.
The rage of an angry storm,
Cannot hide its brilliant light.
Nor can its awesome fury,
Rule as an endless night.
Jesus is the lighthouse,
For those who have gone astray.
The light of His love,
Offers a new and living way.
Jesus is the lighthouse,
When fear and sickness rage.
The light of His love,
Gives hope in difficult days.
So trust in the Lord,
And look for His light.
He alone is "The Lighthouse",
That guides you through the night.

Poem By
John Marinelli

The "Way Maker"

Only Jesus can make a way,
Through the difficulties of life.
He alone is Lord and King,
Over life's sorrows and strife.

He is the "Way Maker,"
When there is no visible way.
He will make the way known,
As though it were the light of day.

He will make a way,
For those of humble heart.
He will clear away the rubble,
Restoring what Satan broke apart.

Jesus is the "Way Maker,"
A friend to all who are lost.
He has made the way,
Paying sin's incredible cost.

The way to the Maker,
Is through His only Son.
He alone is the "Way Maker,"
Until life's battles are won.

Poem By
John Marinelli

Wise Men Still Seek Him

Wise men still seek Him
Who appeared so long ago.
They come now by grace
Through faithful hearts aglow.

Wise men still seek Him
For He is their "Bread of Life."
A sustaining inner strength
Through times of sorrow or strife.

Wise men still seek Him
The Christ of Calvary.
God's only begotten Son
Crucified as Sin's penalty.

Wise men still seek Him
Jesus, God in human array.
King of kings & Lord of lords
Born to earth on Christmas Day.

Poem By
John Marinelli

A Highway Called, "Holiness"

He places my feet on
A highway called "Holiness,"
That led my soul
To the throne of God.

Amidst the cheers of angels,
I walk, wearing His holy gown.
Onward towards heaven's throne,
While evil cast its awful frown.

My eyes were opened
That I might see.
Both the good and the evil,
That sought after me.

I walk the highway-Holiness
That crosses all of time
Towards the throne of God
Leaving this world behind.

Poem By
John Marinelli

Angels Cry "Holy"

The Angels cry "Holy,"
While sorrow fills the land.
For God's Judgment Day,
Is to come upon every man.
The Angels cry "Holy,"
While mankind goes astray,
Rejecting the love of God,
To follow his own precarious way.

The Angels cry "Holy,"
Knowing the terror of the Lord,
When all who dwell in sin,
Will suddenly be destroyed.

The Angels cry "Holy,"
Waiting for all things new,
Born of the Holy Spirit,
When God's Judgment is through.

The Angels cry "Holy,"
"Holy is the Lamb,"
Waiting for the children of God,
To join "The Great I AM"

Poem By
John Marinelli

Call Upon The Lord

When your burdens overwhelm you,
Like a mighty raging sea.
Call upon the Lord, Jesus,
And He will set you free

When your heartaches are many,
And life is difficult to understand.
Call upon the Lord, Jesus.
He will come and hold your hand.

When your friends reject you,
Because you follow after Him,
Call upon the Lord, Jesus.
And keep yourself from sin.

When you fall into depression,
As though it were a giant pit.
Call upon the Lord, Jesus,
Who will restore your joyful wit.

When you're saddened by the day
Feeling lost and all alone.
Call upon the Lord, Jesus,
Who will make His way known.
When you're weary and heavy-laden
Tired from life's many tests.
Call upon the Lord, Jesus
Who is sure to give you rest.

Poem By
John Marinelli

Rest My Child

Come, my child, near to My throne.
Do not allow your faith to roam.
For those who will not believe,
Can never find rest in times of need.

Take your peace and be restored
Then put your faith in Jesus, the Lord
He has provided, your mouth to feed.
From the beginning, He knew your need.
Do not worry, fret or even fear,
for, my child, He is always near.
To bless your soul with love and grace,
To be with you, face to face.

His word shall see you through.
His grace He freely gives to you.
That you should rest, your soul to keep,
Forever delivered from unbelief.

Poem By
John Marinelli

His Call To Glory

Jesus said, "Take up you cross
And follow after me."
His call to Glory,
Is to reject Satan's plea.

We are to lay down our lives,
Even unto the death,
That He may raise us up again
To live with Him in Holiness.
The way up to Glory,
Is the way down in life.
To take up our cross,
Is to avoid anger and strife.

Death to the old man,
Fallen to the nature of sin.
Chosen by the Lord,
To be "Born Again".

So take up your own cross
And follow after Him.
Deny your fallen nature
And be free from the evil within.

Poem By
John Marinelli

A Whisper In The Wind

There's a whisper in the wind
That lingers both day and night.
A champion of truth and justice,
By the power of His might.

A word in due season
That echoes from deep within.
A voice out of nowhere,
Reproving the world of sin.

Look there, in the street
And here, by the shores of the sea.
There's a whisper hidden in the wind;
A voice from eternity.

There's a calling from God.
His voice is hidden in the wind.
In a whisper, He speaks to our hearts
With the love and counsel of a friend.

Listen for the Whisper,
All who seek to know.
It is God's Holy Spirit
Telling you which way to go.

Poem By
John Marinelli

Beyond The Rainbow

I traveled beyond the rainbow
To see all that I could see.
I gazed at the beauty of the stars
And looked straight into eternity.

But when I stood up,
To see if there was more,
I saw the face of Love,
Smiling, as if to adore.

No words were ever spoken
And yet I heard an awesome cry.
A voice that said, "I love you,"
As His shadow drew nigh.

Joy raced around my head
And peace flowed within my soul.
I began to weep and laugh, and shout,
As His presence melted away the cold.

Finally I found forgiveness
From a long and sinful life.
The love of God set me free
From all pain and inward strife.

Poem By
John Marinelli

Fragile Flower Red

As a flower in earthen sod,
I bloom for thee, oh God.
To blossom with the turn of spring;
To be to you, a beautiful thing.

I lift my Fragile Flower Red
Upward from my earthen bed;
To draw light from God above,
Strength and peace and joy and love.

As a flower, I bloom for thee
That passersby may stop and see.
Your fragrance and beauty I am,
Flowered in grace as a man.
As a flower in earthen sod,
I bloom for thee, oh God.
Upward, I lift my head,
As a Fragile Flower Red.

Poem By
John Marinelli

Our Time of Prayer

Oh child of God,
Why do you despair?
My angel's camp
Is around you everywhere.

You may not see
My guiding hand,
Yet I am with you
And I understand.

You are troubled
About so many things.
Your eyes see nothing
Of what my will brings.

Be of good courage
And walk in the light.
Stand up for the truth,
In the power of my might.

For I love you dearly
And will always be there.
Go now my child
Until our next time of prayer.

Poem By
John Marinelli

With Eagle's Wings

I mounted up with "Eagle's Wings"
To soar above the clouds.
I viewed life above its trials,
Separate from the crowds.

Just me and God, together in the day,
His love to behold.
With "Eagle's Wings", He led the way,
My future to unfold.
Forgiveness and peace in a distance,
Suddenly I could see.
Joy and happiness trailed behind
Then overshadowed me.

With "Eagle's Wings" I soared
Above life's every trial.
Now I walk by word of faith,
Rejoicing with every mile.

Poem By
John Marinelli

The Masters Love

In the quiet of the hour,
I walk with my Lord each day.
Sometimes in prayerful thought,
Of what the Master is about to say.
Oft times I sit in silence,
Gazing into heavens door,
Wondering why it was,
That He chose me to adore.
My grace could never compare
With the beauty of the tree.
Why even the flowers
Are greater in stature than me.
Yet He watches over me
With tender loving care.
As a father loves his child,
My Lord is always there.
I listen for His voice,
As His presence draws near.
Knowing that the Masters' love
Will wipe away every tear.

Poem By
John Marinelli

Ask Me Now

Hello my child.
How are you today?
I waited for your call,
And have much to say.
A word in due season,
To cause your faith to soar.
A morsel of truth,
To quiet the lion's roar.
So hear, my beloved,
Before you go on life's way,
And receive a special blessing
By what I have to say.
It's not by might or by power,
That you should gain success.
But by my Holy Spirit
That brings your life's very best.
Ask me now, my child
For all that you need.
For I bless everyone
Who's willing to believe.

Poem By
John Marinelli

Be Still, My Child

Be Still, My Child
Make no sudden sound.
Listen to my earnest plea
Maybe you should sit down.
I've seen your works
Some good and others bad.
For the most part
You've make me sad.
You call upon my name
Only now and then.
Take a quick guess
On how long it's really been.
Prayers were never meant
To be a daily chore.
It was supposed to be our time
For loving fellowship and more.
What will you do
When it's over
And you enter
My glorious light?
You can't bring your riches
Before my heavenly throne.
There is no room for such things.
You'll stand before me all alone.
Will you offer me your wealth?
How about your power or fame?
What are you prepared to give
In exchange for your shame?
Good deeds, though appreciated
Could never free you from sin.
Not to worry, my child

Jesus, my Son, is your friend.
Where you fall short
In prayer, and faith and praise,
Jesus made it right
During His earthly days.
So quit this foolishness
That keeps you bound in fear.
Turn your life over to Jesus
And I'll bring my presence near.
We'll walk together
Through life's every trial,
Dispelling all of your fears
And blessing you with a smile.
The days have all been shortened
That evil may not persist.
Your savior is soon to come
So please do not resist.
Now go your way, my child
To ponder all I've said.
Then come again tonight
As you prepare for bed.
Remember that I love you
And have cleared the way.
But it is all up to you
Whether you follow or stray.

Poem By
John Marinelli

As A Man Thinks, So Is He

I am as my thoughts are,
No matter what you say.
If I think good or bad thoughts,
That is what rules my day.
You cannot know me,
As I really am,
Unless I reveal my thoughts,
And become a transparent man.
You are no different than me,
Underneath all the fleshy show.
We all are as we continually think,
Some happy and others full of woe.
So think on the things in life
That brings out the very best.
And you will surely get better
And be able to finally rest.

Poem By
John Marinelli

Be A Butterfly

Be A Butterfly
And fly away with me.
We'll fly with God's Promises
Straight into eternity.
Be a butterfly
To crawl no more
But to soar in the Spirit
Above earth's mighty roar.
Be a butterfly
To fly to heights unknown,
Soaring on the wings of faith,
Never more to be alone.
Be a butterfly
And fly away with me,
For God has made us new.
At last! At Last! We are free.

Poem By
John Marinelli

ABOUT THE AUTHOR
REV. JOHN MARINELLI

Rev. Marinelli is an ordained minister, He has formed and been pastor of one church in Wisconsin and was the pastor of another in Alabama. He has also been a youth minister and evangelism director over the years.

Rev. Marinelli has authored several books including: "Original Story Poems", a children's story poem book", "The Art of Writing Christian Poetry," "Pulpit Poems," "Moonlight & Mistletoe," "The Mysterious Stranger," and "Mysteries & Miracles."

He is also the author of over 80 short eBook teachings on various Christian subjects. The eBooks are all free downloads from his website;

www.christianliferesourcecenter.org

John is an accomplished Christian poet. He also dabbles in songwriting and writing one act Christian plays.

He is the Vice President of Have A Heart For Companion Animals, Inc., a "No Kill" animal welfare organization. He volunteers his time promoting fundraising events. www.haveaheart.us

Rev. Marinelli is now retired from the sales and marketing arena after spending over 40 years in business-to-business and non-profit marketing.

Rev. Marinelli enjoys writing Christian fiction stories, playing chess, singing karaoke and a retired lifestyle in sunny Florida.

For More Info or eMail Communication
Contact johnmarinelli@embarqmail.com